Little Lem

Written by Rozanne Lanczak Williams
Created by Sue Lewis
Illustrated by Patty Briles

Creative Teaching Press

Little Lemon Lollipops
© 2002 Creative Teaching Press, Inc.
Written by Rozanne Lanczak Williams
Illustrated by Patty Briles
Project Manager: Sue Lewis
Project Director: Carolea Williams

Published in the United States of America by:
Creative Teaching Press, Inc.
P.O. Box 2723
Huntington Beach, CA 92647-0723

ISBN: 1-57471-858-4
CTP 3223

Little lemon lollipops!

Lollipops in a line.

Little lemon lollipops!

The lollipops are mine.

Little lemon lollipops!

I lick them after lunch.

Little lemon lollipops!

I love them very much!

Create your own book!

Decorate a small paper plate to make a lion's head book cover. Use orange and yellow strips of tissue paper for the lion's mane. Cut round paper for the inside pages. Use the frame: *Lion likes _____. Lion likes _____. But Lion loves little lemon lollipops!*

Words in *Little Lemon Lollipops*

Initial Consonant: *l*	High-Frequency Words	Other
little	in	mine
lemon	a	after
lollipops	the	very
line	are	much
lick	I	
lunch	them	
love		